Pandora
the Poodle Fairy

Join the **Rainbow Magic Reading Challenge!**

Read the story and collect your fairy points to climb the
Reading Rainbow at the back of the book.

This book is worth 1 star.

To puppy trainers everywhere

Special thanks to
Rachel Elliot

ORCHARD BOOKS

First published in Great Britain in 2022 by Hodder & Stoughton Limited

3 5 7 9 10 8 6 4

© 2022 Rainbow Magic Limited.
© 2022 HIT Entertainment Limited.
Illustrations © 2022 Hodder & Stoughton Limited.

HIT entertainment

A CIP catalogue record for this book is available from the British Library.

ISBN 978 1 40836 465 9

Printed and bound in Great Britain by Clays Ltd, Elcograf S.p.A

MIX
Paper from
responsible sources
FSC® C104740

The paper and board used in this book are made from wood from responsible sources.

Orchard Books
An imprint of Hachette Children's Group
Part of Hodder & Stoughton Limited
Carmelite House, 50 Victoria Embankment, London EC4Y 0DZ

An Hachette UK Company
www.hachette.co.uk
www.hachettechildrens.co.uk

Pandora
the Poodle Fairy

By Daisy Meadows

ORCHARD

www.orchardseriesbooks.co.uk

Jack Frost's
Ice Castle

Goblin Grotto

High Street

Rachel's
House

TIPPINGTON
TOWN

Jack Frost's Ode

Puppy care sounds dull and dreary.
Training rules just make me weary.
These fairies must be made to see
No puppy matters more than me!

The fairies dared to tell me "no",
So far away their pups will go.
And if they don't do what I say,
I'll yell at them till they obey!

Contents

Chapter One
A Surprise Bundle

"Buttons, fetch!" Rachel Walker called.

Her Old English sheepdog bounded across the park after his ball, which splashed into the stream. Buttons took a flying leap into the water.

"Doggy belly-flop!" exclaimed Rachel's best friend, Kirsty Tate. "Oh no, Buttons,

don't come near me."

But the dog splashed out of the stream, soggy and muddy, and bounded over to drop the ball at Kirsty's feet. Then he shook his shaggy coat, and the girls squealed as they were splattered in icy water.

"Oh Buttons, we're going to have to change our clothes before we go to the shelter," said Rachel, laughing ruefully.

"I look as if I've been jumping in the stream."

The girls had been volunteering at the Leafy Lane Animal Shelter all half term, looking after some newborn puppies that needed special care.

"I thought it was only puppies who were full of bounce," said Kirsty as Rachel clipped on Buttons's lead.

"Buttons always bounces when he sees a stream," said Rachel, laughing. "Come on, let's go back to my house and get changed."

The girls had been spending a lot of time around puppies lately. As well as their volunteer work at the shelter, they had tumbled head first into a magical adventure with some new fairy friends. Li the Labrador Fairy had invited them to the Puppy Care Fair in Fairyland. Everything had gone wrong when Jack Frost had demanded a puppy before he knew how to look after one. When the Puppy Care Fairies said no, he stole their four puppies and magical collars and hid them.

"I keep expecting Pandora the Poodle Fairy to appear at any minute," said Kirsty as they walked back through the park. "Cleo is the only puppy still missing."

"We found all the others," said Rachel, holding on tightly to Buttons's lead. "I know we can find Cleo too. Stop pulling, Buttons."

"I hope we do see Pandora soon," said Kirsty. "She must be worried. Oh!"

She almost fell over as Buttons darted

across the path in front of her.

"Sorry," said Rachel, pulling him back. "It's as if he's forgotten things he's known since he was a puppy."

"I expect it's because Cleo is missing," said Kirsty. "After all, Pandora looks after puppy training. Perhaps older dogs will start to lose their puppy training memories."

Buttons let out a loud woof and dashed forwards, jerking the lead out of Rachel's hand. He hurtled along the path and jumped up at a man who was walking towards them.

"I'm really sorry," said Rachel, hurrying over to him. "Oh, hello Carl!"

The man smiled at both girls over a bundle of blankets in his arms.

"Carl helped us to train Buttons when

he was a puppy," said Rachel. "This is my best friend, Kirsty."

"Hello, Kirsty," said Carl. "Great to see you again, Rachel. How is the lovely Buttons getting on?"

"He's fine, thanks," said Rachel, picking up the lead again. "He's being a bit cheeky this morning but he's usually really good."

"It seems to be that sort of day," said Carl with a grin. "My early-morning puppy training class was a disaster. The owners had forgotten everything and the puppies wouldn't even listen to me."

Rachel and Kirsty shared a hurried glance. They knew exactly why puppy training classes were going wrong.

"I hope things will be better at your next class," said Rachel.

"Thanks," Carl replied with a smile. "I'm on my way to the Leafy Lane Animal Shelter."

"Us too," said Rachel in surprise. "We're volunteering for half term."

"Ah, the newborn puppies," said Carl, nodding. "I heard that the manager had asked for more volunteers. I help out there once a week, advising the manager about what sort of families the animals will suit."

"It'll be interesting to watch you work," said Rachel. "We just have to take Buttons home first."

"I've got some extra work for the manager this morning," said Carl. "Look what I found."

He folded back the edge of the blanket he was carrying, and a huge pair of trusting eyes looked up at the girls. A little pink tongue licked Carl's hand.

"She's a friendly young lady," Carl said.

The little dog's eyes were gunky, and her coat was matted with leaves and mud.

"Poor little thing," said Kirsty, gently stroking her head.

"Maybe you two could help to clean her up," Carl suggested.

"We'd love to," said Rachel. "Come on, Buttons, Kirsty and I have got work to do!"

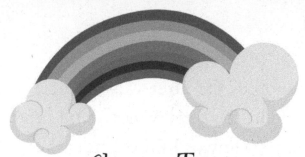

Chapter Two
News for Pandora

When Rachel and Kirsty arrived at
the shelter, they went straight to the
kennel where the newborn puppies were
sleeping. There was a lot to do. The
girls started by feeding them with milk
substitute. Then the puppies needed to be
burped and helped to go to the toilet.

As soon as the litter was sleeping peacefully, the girls went to find Nate, the manager. He was in the garden behind the shelter, watching Carl work with a greyhound who had been left at the shelter the day before. Several older dogs were sniffing around the grass, and the puppy that Carl had found was finishing a bowl of food beside him.

"We've fed the puppies and put the dirty towels and blankets in the washing machine," said Kirsty. "What would you like us to do next?"

Nate smiled down at her.

"That's great work," he said. "I believe you've already met our newest arrival. We've fed her, but she needs to be thoroughly washed and groomed. Would you be able to do that?"

"We'd love to," said Kirsty.

"I've bathed Buttons lots of times," Rachel added.

Nate showed them an old tin bath filled with warm water. Beside

it was a soft puppy bed, a bottle of dog shampoo, a thick towel, a comb and some pet wipes. A hose lay on the grass beside them.

"Make sure you dry her really well afterwards," he said. "The sunshine will do the rest."

He went to help Carl, and the girls carefully placed the dirty puppy into the warm water. She stood still as they massaged shampoo through her tangled coat.

"She's so sweet," said Rachel. "I think she knows that we're trying to help her."

Slowly, the water in the bath became darker. Kirsty picked up the hose and turned on a gentle spray of warm water.

"I'll rinse her face by hand while you do her body," said Rachel.

"It looks as if she's chocolate brown," said Kirsty after a few moments. "It was hard to tell before."

"I'm sure I've met her," Rachel said. "Maybe I've seen her with her owner in the park."

"She looks familiar to me too," said Kirsty. "Do you think she's a poodle?"

"I know who she reminds me of," said

Rachel suddenly. "She looks just like Cleo."

The girls stared at one another and then back at the puppy. Could this really be Pandora's magical puppy? They had seen her a few days ago at the Puppy Care Fair, but they hadn't met her close up.

"Is it possible?" whispered Kirsty.

Rachel lifted the puppy out of the bath and wrapped her in the towel.

"Cleo?" she said.

The dog looked up at her eagerly and let out a little yip.

"I'm sure it's her," said Rachel, tingling with surprise and excitement. "This is wonderful! Now all we have to do is take her back to Pandora and everything will go back to normal."

"But how are we going to get her to Fairyland?" asked Kirsty, glancing around at Carl and Nate. "We can't use our fairy dust in front of them. They would be sure to notice."

During their adventures with the Weather Fairies, the girls had each been given a special locket by Queen Titania. There was just enough fairy dust inside each one for a trip to Fairyland.

Wondering what to do next, the girls

combed Cleo's silky coat and used the
wipes to clean her ears. As they were
checking her paws, Carl's voice carried
over the grass to them.

"Remember, distract him from
behaviour you don't like," he was telling
Nate. "Use a toy to get his attention and
play with him."

"That's it," said Rachel. "We need a
distraction."

She still had a pocket full of dog treats
from their walk with Buttons. Giving
Cleo to Kirsty, she took a big handful of
treats and made sure that the older dogs
in the garden could see her. They came
running over. Nate and Carl still weren't
looking.

"Now," Kirsty whispered.

Rachel threw the treats to the far side

of the garden as hard as she could. There was instant and total pandemonium as all the dogs belted across the garden. Woofing and yipping, they zoomed past Carl and Nate and nearly knocked them down.

"What's the matter with them?" Nate asked.

"We'd better go and check," said Carl.

As the men jogged after the dogs,
Rachel and Kirsty wrapped their arms
around Cleo and opened their lockets.
A helpful breeze blew the fairy dust over
them, and they shrank to fairy size at
once.

"Find Pandora," said Rachel.

Cleo whined.

"Don't worry," Kirsty whispered in
Cleo's ear. "We're taking you home."

Chapter Three
Good News and Bad News

There was a burst of sparkling stars all around, as dazzling as fireworks. Every colour of the rainbow danced before their eyes. They clung together as they whirled away from the human world.

Cleo whined in alarm as the sparkles and stars grew more vibrant. Then, in the blink of an eye, they were standing in a little meadow filled with lush green grass. They fluttered their gauzy wings and shared a smile of breathless happiness.

"We're back in Fairyland," said Rachel.

"But where in Fairyland?" Kirsty wondered. "Do you think we've come to the right place?"

There was a wooden cabin behind them, and the girls peeped inside.

"Wow, it's puppy paradise," said Rachel. "I think we've definitely come to the right place."

There were boxes of puppy treats, low climbing frames, colourful plastic cones, leads hanging from hooks on the walls and water bowls in every corner. Chew toys were scattered around the floor.

"Do you remember it here, Cleo?"

Kirsty asked the cuddly pup.

Suddenly, Cleo started to bark. Still holding her, Kirsty whirled around and saw all four of the Puppy Care Fairies walking across the far end of the meadow. Pandora looked up when she heard her puppy and let out a squeal of excitement.

"Cleo!" she cried.

Kirsty let Cleo go, and the puppy zoomed towards her owner. Half laughing and half crying, Pandora scooped the wagging, licking, wiggling Cleo into her arms. Her blonde curls bounced as she buried her face in Cleo's soft coat.

At last she looked up at Rachel and Kirsty. Happy tears were shining in her brown eyes, magnified by her glasses. She was wearing a simple white T-shirt and a pair of denim shorts with brown boots.

"Thank you from the very bottom of my heart," she whispered. "How ever did

you manage to find her?"

"She found us," said Kirsty, and explained how they had met Carl that morning.

The other Puppy Care Fairies gathered around, hugging Rachel and Kirsty. Their puppies, Buddy, Pepper and Wiggles, bounded over to say hello too.

"This is better than I could have hoped for," said Pandora. "I wonder how she escaped. You clever girl, Cleo!"

"She was very dirty, but we've washed and combed her," said Rachel.

"Thank you," said Pandora again. "Oh, where's her collar?"

Rachel and Kirsty felt as if the sun had gone behind a cloud. They exchanged a nervous glance.

"We didn't even think about her collar," said Rachel in a small voice.

"We're sorry," said Kirsty.

Pandora had gone very pale. Cleo's magical blue collar and silver whistle dog tag helped her to watch over puppy training everywhere.

"It's wonderful that Cleo is safe," she said. "But I have to find her collar.

Without it, even experienced dog trainers will be unable to train a single puppy."

"Please let us help you," said Rachel at once.

Kirsty took Pandora's hand, and the little fairy smiled at them gratefully.

"That would be wonderful," she said.

"We'll take care of Cleo," said Li at once. "Where are you going to start looking?"

"Do you think the collar could be in Jack Frost's castle?" Frenchie asked.

"I think we should go back to the human world and ask Carl exactly where he found Cleo," said Kirsty. "Maybe that will give us a clue."

"Good thinking," said Seren. "And good luck, all of you."

With a tap of her wand, Pandora

refilled the magical lockets. Then she
whispered a spell, and the training field
seemed to disappear in a swirl of silvery
mist.

Chapter Four
A Woodland Trail

When the silvery mist cleared, the girls
were human again.

"We're back at the shelter," said Rachel,
looking around.

The older dogs were still racing towards
the treats she had thrown. Of course, no
time had passed in the human world

while they had been in Fairyland.
Pandora swooped under a lock of Kirsty's
hair to hide.

"Oh my goodness, what are we going
to tell Carl and Nate about Cleo?" asked
Kirsty suddenly. "They're bound to notice
that she's not here."

Rachel raced into the shelter and
came out with an armful of towels and
blankets. Quickly, she bundled them up
in the puppy bed.

"Hopefully they'll think she's asleep
under there," she said.

She was just in time. Carl walked
towards them and looked at the filthy
water in the bath.

"It looks as if you did a great job," he
said. "I bet she felt better after that. How
is she doing?"

"She seems happy," said Kirsty, truthfully.

Carl glanced at the pile of blankets.

"I won't disturb her," he said. "We'll let her sleep."

"Where exactly did you find her?" asked Rachel as they walked away from the puppy bed.

"She was hiding in the little tunnel where the stream enters the park," he replied. "I heard her whimpering as I walked past. Her family must be worried about her. If only she had been wearing a collar."

"I know where that tunnel is," said Rachel. "We should go and hunt for clues."

"That's a good idea," said Carl. "I'll let Nate know where you've gone."

The girls left the shelter and headed back to the park.

"I feel a bit bad," said Rachel, panting. "Carl thinks we're looking for clues to her owner, and that's not the truth."

"We didn't tell him anything that wasn't true," said Kirsty. "Besides, if we don't find that collar, Carl won't be able to do his job. I don't think you should feel bad."

Rachel flashed her a grateful smile. Her best friend always knew how to make her feel better.

It didn't take them long to reach the tunnel. There was no one around, so Pandora flew out from under Kirsty's hair and hovered inside the tunnel.

"Goodness, I can see why Cleo was so dirty," said Kirsty, peeping inside.

The tunnel was thick with mud and leaves. Any clues would have sunk into the brown slime.

But outside the tunnel, where the bank of the stream was firmer, Rachel spotted something.

"Footprints," she said, pointing.

Pandora swooped down to look at them. They were large and barefoot.

"Not just ordinary footprints," she said. "Goblin footprints!"

The footprints criss-crossed each other, broken up

with dents in the mud where a goblin must have fallen down.

"They must have had a scuffle here," said Rachel. "Perhaps this is where Cleo got away from them."

At first it was hard to see where the prints led, but at last Kirsty saw a set leading away from the stream towards a little patch of woodland.

"We have to track them," said Rachel.

Pandora flew ahead into the wood, and the girls followed as quickly as they

could, scrunching through old leaves and twigs. Even though it was a sunny day, the trees made it dark.

"It's a bit creepy in here," said Rachel, when they had been walking for a few minutes. "I've never thought that before."

"It's because there are no birds singing," said Pandora, rising up into the air and looking all around. "And that, my friends, is a hopeful sign. Goblins often frighten birds away when they're being extra boisterous."

"Let's stop walking," Kirsty suggested. "Our feet are making a lot of noise. Let's stand still and listen."

Rachel and Kirsty stood as still as the trees, and Pandora landed lightly on Rachel's head. It took a moment, but then they heard it.

"It's your fault, nincompoop," squawked an angry voice.

"Leave me alone, fish-face," shouted someone else.

There was a scuffle and then muffled, squabbling voices.

"That's them," said Pandora in an urgent whisper. "Come on!"

Chapter Five
Puppies Galore!

Pandora zoomed ahead, and the girls followed as quietly as they could. After a few minutes, they saw three goblins sitting underneath an oak tree and hurling insults at each other.

"It's not my fault," a scowling goblin was saying. "No one told me that puppies could be so wriggly."

"Everyone knows puppies are wriggly,"
said another goblin scornfully. "You're
just a dimwit."

"Stop bickering and think," said the
third goblin. "We've still got the collar. We
just have to get another puppy."

"How can we get a puppy?" squealed
the first goblin, waving his arms around
hysterically. "We can't afford to buy one."

"Are you a goblin or a goat?" asked
the third goblin, curling his lip. "We
don't have to buy one. There are loads
of people walking their dogs in the park
over there. We'll just take one of those
and put the collar on it. Jack Frost won't
notice."

"But how can we snatch it off the
owner?" asked the second goblin.

"Humans are funny about their dogs. They might try to stop us."

"I'll talk to the owner while you two get the dog to follow you," said the third goblin.

"This is awful," said Rachel. "They're planning to steal someone's family pet!"

"But what would attract a puppy?" asked the first goblin.

"Do I have to think of everything?" snapped the third goblin. "Turn your brain on! Bogmallows? Iceberry pops? Just find something and then stick the dog in this and let's go."

He threw a heavy sack at the others.

"A sack?" whispered Pandora. "How horrible. That would really frighten a puppy. It would take months of training to help them recover."

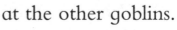

"The poor owner would be frightened too," said Rachel. "How are we going to stop them?"

Still squabbling, the goblins scrambled to their feet.

"They're getting ready to go," Kirsty exclaimed. "We have to do something right now."

The third goblin waved something blue at the other goblins. There was a flash of silver and Pandora gasped.

"That's it," she cried out. "That's Cleo's magical collar."

Suddenly, a wonderful idea

popped into Rachel's head.

"Quickly, Pandora, use your magic to turn us into puppies," she said. "We can run around the goblins and confuse them. They won't try to steal someone's pet when there are three poodle puppies in front of them."

"Yes, and then one of us could snatch the collar and run away," said Kirsty. "Brilliant idea!"

Pandora waved her wand and a trail of silver sparkles streamed around them as she spoke the words of a spell.

"Let a magic change occur;
Hide our true selves under fur.
Floppy ears and curly hair,
To save the day with puppy flair!"

Rachel and Kirsty felt themselves shrinking, and their hands and feet turned into furry paws. Each of them grew a fluffy tail, which started wagging immediately. Hundreds of new and amazing smells hit their senses, and they sniffed the air in amazement.

"I can hear the sound of birds' wings flapping up above," said Rachel.

At least, that was what she meant to say. What actually came out of her mouth was: *WOOF! WOOF! WOOFITY-WOOF!*

Pandora had turned into a white poodle pup. Rachel was golden and Kirsty was dark brown. Kirsty yipped, and they all ran towards the goblins.

"Hey, look," squawked the first goblin. "Puppies galore!"

Rachel, Kirsty and Pandora zoomed around and through the goblins' legs. They could never have run so fast as humans. Suddenly Rachel understood why Buttons had loved zooming around the garden when he was a puppy. She opened her mouth to laugh and her long dog tongue lolled out.

"Catch them!" the third goblin was howling. "Stop them! Turn around!"

The collar was dangling from his hand as he ordered the other two about. They panicked and ran straight into each other at full pelt. *THUMP!* They landed hard on the twiggy floor.

"YOWCH!"

Pandora and Kirsty jumped over them as if they were hurdles.

"Idiots!" the third goblin hollered.

He wasn't looking at the puppies because he was too busy shouting at the other goblins. This was their chance! Rachel gathered up all her strength and leapt through the air, snatching the collar with her needle-sharp puppy teeth. Yes!

She skidded to a halt and turned, ready to run. But at that second, there was

a deafening *CRACK!* and a flash of
blue lightning. Suddenly, Jack Frost was
standing in front of her.

"Not so fast," he snarled.

He grabbed her by the scruff of her
neck and yanked the collar from her
mouth.

"That's mine!" he hissed.

There was another flash of lightning,
and Jack Frost had disappeared . . . with
Rachel.

Chapter Six
A Little Tied Up!

The goblins had all flung themselves face down when they saw Jack Frost, so they hadn't realised he had vanished again. Pandora, who was holding her wand in her mouth, used it to return herself and Kirsty back to their normal selves. Kirsty's tummy felt as if it was turning over.

Where was her best friend?

"We can follow him," said Pandora. "Because Rachel was enchanted by me, I can track her magical trail."

The goblins sat up.

"Where did you two come from?" asked the third goblin. "And where are those puppies?"

Pandora frowned and pointed her wand at the sack, which promptly disappeared.

"Never do anything like that again," she said. "Puppies are living creatures, just like you. They can feel fear and pain, just like you. How would you like to be dropped in a sack and carried away from everyone you know?"

"I wouldn't like that at all," said the first goblin in a small voice.

"Exactly," said Pandora, giving them

all a stern look. "Come on, Kirsty. Let's follow Rachel."

She held Kirsty's hand, and they were caught up in a glittering puff of silver sparkles. When the sparkles cleared, they were back in the meadow with the wooden cabin.

"This is my training field," said

Pandora, sounding confused. "Why has he brought Rachel here?"

Jack Frost was standing in front of the cabin with Rachel, still in puppy form, under his arm. The other Puppy Care Fairies were a short distance away, looking shocked.

"Give me one of your puppies," he demanded. "I know that this isn't one of yours."

Pandora flicked her wand, and Rachel transformed into a fairy.

"Fly, Rachel!" Pandora called out.

Rachel tried, but Jack Frost sent a bolt of blue lightning at her back. She froze like an ice cube and she fell at his feet.

"Let her go!" Kirsty shouted.

"Not until I get a real puppy with its real collar," Jack Frost said in a low,

hissing tone. "Feel free to discuss who loses their pup. I've got plenty of time."

The fairies huddled together and spoke in low voices.

"What are we going to do?" asked Seren.

"We can't give any of the puppies up," said Li. "But we can't leave Rachel with Jack Frost either."

Kirsty noticed that the puppies were huddling together too. She could hear

them yipping. The fairies had dropped
their leads in shock. Suddenly, the yipping
stopped. Buddy, Pepper, Cleo and Wiggles
nodded at each other. Then they turned
and raced towards Jack Frost. Around and
around his ankles they zoomed, making
him spin in circles.

"You clever puppies," Kirsty whispered.

"Control your dogs!" Jack Frost yelled
at the fairies.

"Oh, just this once, I don't think so,"
said Pandora, with a little smile.

Dizzy and disorientated from spinning,
Jack Frost fell sideways with a loud
CRASH! At once, Wiggles pounced on
his hand and snatched his wand. Cleo
seized her collar from his other hand,
while Pepper and Buddy sat on his chest
and yipped triumphantly.

"Good dogs!" the fairies chorused.

A light tap of Pandora's wand melted the ice around Rachel. Then Kirsty put Cleo's collar back around her silky neck.

"Thank you," said Pandora. "At last, puppy training can return to normal."

"Get off," Jack Frost wailed, drumming his heels on the ground. "I've changed my mind. I can't stand puppies and I never want to see another one as long as I live."

"What will happen to him?" asked
Rachel.

"I'm sure the king and queen will want
to speak to him before they return his
wand," said Pandora. "Until they arrive,
I think we should show him a few puppy
training lessons. It would be amazing if
he could learn how much fun it is to be a
good dog owner."

"That's a great idea," said Kirsty. "We
should get back to the shelter. What
are we going to say to Carl and Nate?
They'll want to know where Cleo went."

Pandora shook her curly head.

"Cleo is touched with fairy magic,"
she said. "They won't remember her now
that she has been returned and we've
got her collar back. Thank you, Rachel
and Kirsty. I will never forget that you

brought Cleo home to me."

"We all want to thank you," said Li, holding out her arms.

They joined in a group hug, their gossamer wings fluttering together. Rachel and Kirsty laughed as they felt little puppy licks on their legs.

"The puppies say 'thank you' too," said Seren, laughing.

Swirls of rainbow-bright fairy dust hid the meadow and the fairies from view, and the girls blinked. They were standing in the garden behind the Leafy Lane Animal Shelter. Carl and Nate were playing with a shaggy German shepherd, and Rachel checked her watch.

"It's time for the puppies to have their next feed," she said.

"Now that we've stopped Jack Frost, we can really relax and enjoy looking after them," said Kirsty.

"There's just one problem left," said Rachel, smiling. "How ever are we going to stop ourselves from taking all those sweet little puppies home?"

The End

Now it's time for Kirsty and
Rachel to help...

Kat the Jungle Fairy

Read on for a sneak peek...

"Here we are at last, boys and girls,"
said Mrs Hauxwell over the coach's
microphone. "Welcome to Jungle World."

Rachel Walker and her school friends
gazed at the entrance to Jungle World
with their noses pressed against the coach
windows.

"It took a long time to get here from
Tippington School," said Mila, who was
sitting in the seat beside Rachel.

"It was worth it," said Rachel, with a
grin. "This is going to be the best day
ever."

Not only was Jungle World an amazing

theme park and zoo, but Rachel's best friend, Kirsty Tate, was meeting her there. Both their schools were there to celebrate the end of term. They had been doing projects about the jungle for weeks.

"Mum arranged it all with Mrs Hauxwell," said Rachel. "I'm going to go round Jungle World with Kirsty's school group, so we can spend the day together."

"That's brilliant," said Mila. "You must miss her. I expect it's really hard that your best friend goes to a different school."

"Our adventures together make up for it," said Rachel, with a little smile.

She and Kirsty shared a secret that had made their friendship even better. They were friends with the fairies! When they were together, magical adventures always seemed to be just around the corner.

Mila smiled back at Rachel. She was a tall girl with dark hair and friendly eyes that twinkled beneath a swishy fringe. As the coach stopped, Rachel noticed Mila's pink nail varnish and grinned. Nail varnish wasn't usually allowed at school, but the rules were different on the last day of term.

A crowd of schoolchildren was standing at the entrance to Jungle World.

"There's Kirsty," said Rachel, spotting her best friend among them.

She waved and Kirsty waved back, beaming from ear to ear. At the front of the coach, Mrs Hauxwell laughed.

"Go on, Rachel," she said, opening the coach door. "Go ahead and meet your friend. We'll see you back here at the end of the day."

Kirsty ran to meet Rachel as she jumped off the coach.

"Aren't we lucky?" Kirsty cried, throwing her arms around Rachel and giving her a big hug. "I'm so excited that we're here on the same day. There are lots of things to see and do."

"I know," said Rachel, taking Kirsty's hand. "I've been reading about the amazing birds on Parrot Island, and I can't wait to visit Jungle Paths. It's supposed to be just like the natural habitat of Madagascar."

"I want to visit Reptile Encounter," said Kirsty. "And if we've got time, there's Jungle Adventure."

"Ooh, is that the outdoor adventure zone?" Rachel asked. "I heard they've got zip lines and high ropes and—"

"Attention please, everyone," called Kirsty's teacher. "I can hear a lot of chatter about all the wonderful places you want to visit. You're free to explore, but I expect to see every single one of you at the Flamingo Café at lunchtime."

"Yes, sir!" called out forty voices.

"Please can we go to Jungle Paths first?" Rachel begged. "I've been learning all about Madagascar, and I can't wait to see all the incredible creatures face to face. I just hope we see a lemur. They're so shy that they might hide away from us."

Jungle Paths was everything that Rachel had hoped. Inside a white dome, she and Kirsty strolled under low tree canopies, treading on mosses, lichens and ferns. The air felt heavy with moisture.

Red frogs, yellow moths and bright chameleons peered at them from trees and bushes.

"I'm surprised it's so chilly," said Kirsty. "I thought Madagascar was a warm, humid place."

"It is," Rachel replied. "This habitat should be exactly the same, to keep the animals and plants happy."

Kirsty shivered and rubbed her arms.

"I think it's getting colder," she said.

Suddenly, the leaves in front of them parted, and they saw a small furry animal gazing at them. It had large, shining eyes surrounded with black circles, and a tail ringed in black and white.

"A lemur," whispered Rachel in wonder. "It's beautiful."

The lemur raised a paw and beckoned to them. The girls exchanged an astonished glance.

"Did you see that?" Kirsty asked.

Rachel nodded, just as the lemur beckoned again.

There was no one else nearby. The girls stepped through the fronds and wet leaves and saw a little fairy hidden among the plants.

The fairy smiled at them.

"Hi," she said. "I'm Kat the Jungle Fairy."

She was wearing a leopard-print top and a skirt made from green jungle fronds. Colourful orchids decorated her hair and waist, and she wore a bracelet of delicate leaves around her wrist.

"It's wonderful to meet you, Kat," said

Kirsty. "We had no idea that we were going to see a fairy today."

"I had no idea that I was going to see you, either," said Kat. "When I spotted you walking past, I knew that luck was on my side. You see, I look after tropical jungles in the fairy and human worlds, and all the plants and animals inside them. I'm here because Jack Frost and his goblins have stolen my magical objects."

"Oh no, that's awful," said Rachel. "What brought you here?"

"I chased the goblins here, but then I lost sight of them among the plants," Kat explained. "I was just asking the lemurs if they had seen anything when I spotted you. I recognised you at once. Everyone knows what Fairyland's best friends look like! Please, will you help me to track down the goblins? They are definitely somewhere here in Jungle World."

"Of course we'll help," said Kirsty. "You don't have to do this on your own. But what have the goblins stolen? Tell us about your magical objects."

Kat waved her wand, and several plants leaned in towards each other, holding out their leaves to make a screen. Kat tapped the leafy screen with her wand, and a picture appeared. It was a small, shining object that looked a little like an old-fashioned pocket watch.

"This is the golden sundial," said Kat. "It keeps the weather correct for different jungle environments around the world."

The picture of the golden sundial faded and was replaced by a little green basket.

"This is the green garden basket," Kat

said. "It makes sure that there is enough food for each jungle animal."

The picture faded, and a beautiful flower appeared.

"This is the red orchid," Kat told them. "It protects the jungle from the outside world."

The picture of the flower seemed to melt away, and the plants stood up straight again.

"Why did Jack Frost take them?" asked Rachel.

"Yesterday I told him off for letting goblins play in the jungle," said Kat. "They were being very naughty, riding on a warthog's back and trampling all over the rare plants. He wants to pay me back for daring to tell him off. But by taking my objects, he's punishing the animals and plants in my care. I *have* to save them."

Rachel and Kirsty could see the determination in Kat's eyes.

"You're really brave," said Kirsty. "Not everyone has the courage to stand up to Jack Frost."

Read Kat the Jungle Fairy to
find out what adventures are in store for Kirsty and Rachel!

Calling all parents, carers and teachers!
The Rainbow Magic fairies are here to help
your child enter the magical world of reading.
Whatever reading stage they are at, there's
a Rainbow Magic book for everyone!
Here is Lydia the Reading Fairy's guide to
supporting your child's journey at all levels.

Starting Out
Our Rainbow Magic Beginner Readers are perfect for first-time readers who are just beginning to develop reading skills and confidence. Approved by teachers, they contain a full range of educational levelling, as well as lively full-colour illustrations.

Developing Readers
Rainbow Magic Early Readers contain longer stories and wider vocabulary for building stamina and growing confidence. These are adaptations of our most popular Rainbow Magic stories, specially developed for younger readers in conjunction with an Early Years reading consultant, with full-colour illustrations.

Going Solo
The Rainbow Magic chapter books - a mixture of series and one-off specials - contain accessible writing to encourage your child to venture into reading independently. These highly collectible and much-loved magical stories inspire a love of reading to last a lifetime.

www.orchardseriesbooks.co.uk

"Rainbow Magic got my daughter reading chapter books. Great sparkly covers, cute fairies and traditional stories full of magic that she found impossible to put down" - Mother of Edie (6 years)

"Florence LOVES the Rainbow Magic books. She really enjoys reading now" - Mother of Florence (6 years)

Read along the Reading Rainbow!

Well done – you have completed the book!

This book was worth 1 star.

See how far you have climbed on the Reading Rainbow opposite.
The more books you read, the more stars you can colour in
and the closer you will be to becoming a Royal Fairy!

Do you want to print your own Reading Rainbow?

1) Go to the Rainbow Magic website

2) Download and print out the poster

3) Colour in a star for every book you finish
and climb the Reading Rainbow

4) For every step up the rainbow,
you can download your very own certificate

There's all this and lots more at
orchardseriesbooks.co.uk

You'll find activities, stories, a special newsletter
AND you can search for the fairy with your name!